Look and Find

Fairy Tales

Snow White • Goldilocks
Little Mermaid • Sleeping Beauty
Three Little Pigs • And more!

Illustrated by Jerry Tiritilli

Illustration script development by David Guy Martino

Louis Weber, C.E.O.
Publications International, Ltd.
7373 North Cicero Avenue
Lincolnwood, Illinois 60646

Manufactured in the U.S.A.

8 7 6 5 4 3 2 1

ISBN 1-56173-420-9

PUBLICATIONS INTERNATIONAL, LTD.

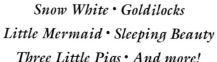
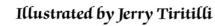
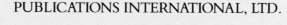

GRAUMAN'S CHINESE THEATRE

The Prince must find the young lady whose foot fits the little glass slipper he found. Can you help the Prince find Cinderella?

Look for the fellows below, too. Help them find *their* true loves. Their darling damsels are also missing one shoe!

Cinderella

Frank N. Stein

Long John Silver

Joe Bowler

Surfer Doodz

Rex Rodeo

Bob E. Soxer

I. C. Skater

CORN -O- COPIA

SHOE THRU WAY

HELP WANTED

TOES R US

TOE ROAD

When the Three Little Pigs grew up, they started Bacon Bros. Construction Company. They built lots of famous buildings!

Can you find the Three Little Pigs? Do you see the Big Bad Wolf? Have fun looking for these buildings, too!

Francis Bacon

Quisp Bacon

Fats Bacon

Big Bad Wolf

The "Ears" Tower

The "Eye-Ful" Tower

The Leaning Tower of "Pizza"

Banished to the woods for being so beautiful, Snow White took refuge at the Seven Dwarfs Hotel. The Wicked Queen is still looking for Snow White, though.

Find the Seven Dwarfs so they can warn Snow White about the Queen. Find Snow White, too!

Snow White

Blip

Glitch

Bit

Byte

Fuss

Fidget

Bonsai

Little Red Riding Hood is going to visit her granny on the other side of the forest. Her path is full of danger! There are many Big Bad Wolves who would like to have Little Red for supper!

First find Little Red and her granny. Then look for these dangers throughout the forest.

Little Red

Granny

A wolf with a net

A wolf with a rope

A wolf with dynamite

A wolf with a sack

A wolf in disguise

A wolf with a slingshot

There's been a break-in. Some porridge is missing, a chair is broken, beds are slept-in. We have an idea "whodunit." A kid named Goldilocks has been seen in the area. We know one thing for sure: She has bad manners.

I'm Sgt. Thursday. Will you help me find these characters and clues at the scene of the crime?

Goldilocks

Papa Bear

Mama Bear

Baby Bear

A broken chair

Detective Sure-Lock Homes

Lt. Clod-dumbo

Goldilocks' ribbon

Life in Neptune's kingdom went swimmingly until the Little Mermaid saved the Prince's life. She has fallen head over fins in love—and even wishes she were human!

First, find the Little Mermaid. Next, look for these human things that mermaids cannot use.

The Little Mermaid

A pair of pants

A bicycle

Panty hose

Sneakers

A pogo stick

Socks

Roller skates

Once the wicked witch was gone, Hansel and Gretel started eating up the gingerbread house. But there were so many goodies, they invited all their friends to join in the fun!

After you find Hansel and Gretel, look for these *sweet* kids!

Hansel

Gretel

Cinnamon-Swirl Pearl

Cotton-Candy Andy

Lolly Popp

Gingerbread Fred

Bubbles Gumm

Chip Chocolate

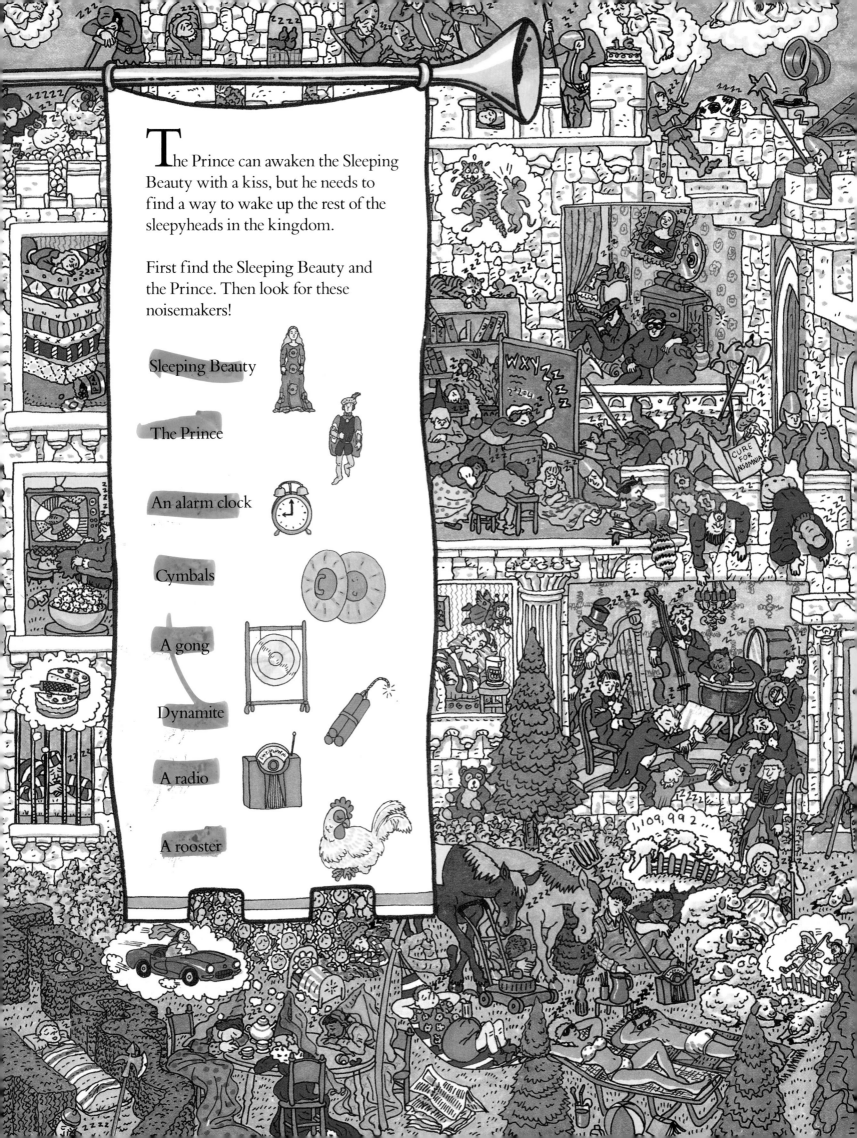

The Prince can awaken the Sleeping Beauty with a kiss, but he needs to find a way to wake up the rest of the sleepyheads in the kingdom.

First find the Sleeping Beauty and the Prince. Then look for these noisemakers!

Sleeping Beauty

The Prince

An alarm clock

Cymbals

A gong

Dynamite

A radio

A rooster

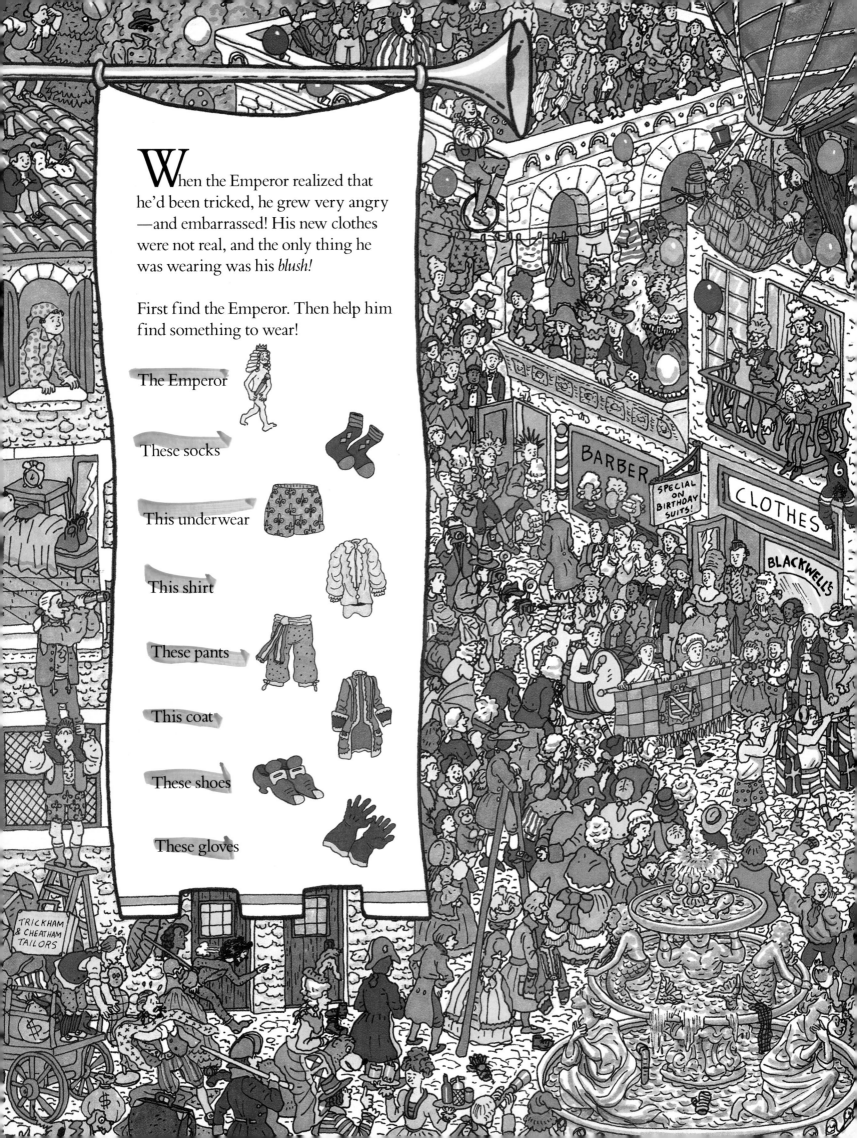

When the Emperor realized that he'd been tricked, he grew very angry —and embarrassed! His new clothes were not real, and the only thing he was wearing was his *blush!*

First find the Emperor. Then help him find something to wear!

The Emperor

These socks

This underwear

This shirt

These pants

This coat

These shoes

These gloves

Turn back to the Emperor's parade. Can you find these other bare—and bear—things?

- ☐ A polar bear
- ☐ A bear hug . . .
- ☐ . . . and a *bare* hug!
- ☐ Bare feet . . .
- ☐ . . . and *bear* feet!
- ☐ A bear rug
- ☐ A teddy bear
- ☐ A bareback rider . . .
- ☐ . . . and a *bearback* rider!

Sleeping Beauty slept through her sixteenth birthday. Can you find these slumber party things?

- ☐ A sleeping bag
- ☐ A birthday cake
- ☐ A bowl of popcorn
- ☐ A bottle of soda pop
- ☐ A record player
- ☐ Fluffy bedroom slippers
- ☐ A princess phone
- ☐ A teddy bear

There are plenty of fish in the sea! Help the Little Mermaid find these.

- ☐ A "star" fish
- ☐ A "sun" fish
- ☐ A hammerhead shark
- ☐ A flying fish
- ☐ A "cat" fish
- ☐ An "angel" fish
- ☐ A "holey" mackerel
- ☐ A card shark
- ☐ A pool shark

Go back to the Bear place to look for these police things:

- ☐ A star-shaped badge
- ☐ Three nightsticks
- ☐ A magnifying glass
- ☐ A bullhorn
- ☐ A wanted poster
- ☐ A chalk outline
- ☐ A parking ticket
- ☐ A walkie-talkie
- ☐ A pair of handcuffs